Welcome to ALADDIN QUIX!

If you are looking for fast, fun-to-read stories with colorful characters, lots of kid-friendly humor, easy-to-follow action, entertaining story lines, and lively illustrations, then **ALADDIN QUIX** is for you!

But wait, there's more!

If you're also looking for stories with tables of contents; word lists; about-the-book questions; 64, 80, or 96 pages; short chapters; short paragraphs; and large fonts, then **ALADDIN QUIX** is *definitely* for you!

ALADDIN QUIX: The next step between ready to reads and longer, more challenging chapter books, for readers five to eight years old.

THE GIANTS
GO CAMPING

Read more **ALADDIN QUIX** books!

Giants

By Jane Yolen

Book 1: *The Giants' Farm*

THE
GIANTS
GO CAMPING

BY
Jane Yolen

ILLUSTRATED BY
Tomie dePaola

ALADDIN QUIX

New York London Toronto Sydney New Delhi

This book is a work of fiction. Any references to historical events, real people, or real places are used fictitiously. Other names, characters, places, and events are products of the author's imagination, and any resemblance to actual events or places or persons, living or dead, is entirely coincidental.

ALADDIN QUIX

Simon & Schuster Children's Publishing Division

1230 Avenue of the Americas, New York, New York 10020

First Aladdin QUIX paperback edition September 2023

Text copyright © 1979 by Jane Yolen

Illustrations copyright © 1979 by Tomie dePaola

Also available in an Aladdin QUIX hardcover edition.

All rights reserved, including the right of reproduction in whole or in part in any form.

ALADDIN and the related marks and colophon are trademarks of Simon & Schuster, Inc.

For information about special discounts for bulk purchases, please contact

Simon & Schuster Special Sales at 1-866-506-1949 or business@simonandschuster.com.

The Simon & Schuster Speakers Bureau can bring authors to your live event. For more information or to book an event contact the Simon & Schuster Speakers Bureau at 1-866-248-3049 or visit our website at www.simonspeakers.com.

Designed by Karin Paprocki

The text of this book was set in Archer Medium.

Manufactured in the United States of America 0723 OFF

2 4 6 8 10 9 7 5 3 1

Library of Congress Control Number 2023933127

ISBN 9781534488618 (hc)

ISBN 9781534488601 (pbk)

ISBN 9781534488625 (ebook)

For Adam, Betsy, Ari, and Wee David, who is now BIG,

plus Peter B. Tacy, who makes me happy

—J. Y.

Cast of Characters

Grizzle: The biggest giant, who builds things

Dazzle: The roundest giant, who likes to cook

Grab: Grub's twin, who shares secrets

Grub: Grab's twin, who shares secrets

Dab: The smallest giant, who reads books and solves problems

Contents

Vacation Time

It was summer at Fe-Fi-Fo-Farm.

It was hot in the fields where **Grizzle**, the biggest, plowed.

It was hot in the kitchen where **Dazzle** cooked.

It was hot in the barn where **Grab** and **Grub** cleaned.

It was hot in the den where little **Dab** wrote.

And it got hotter and hotter.

"It is too hot to work," said Dab. "It is time to go on **vacation**."

The other giants agreed.

"Someplace cool," said Grizzle.

He wiped his face with a big hand.

"Someplace wet," said the twins. They were covered with dirt.

"Someplace where there is lots to eat," said Dazzle.

So Dab sat down and thought. *Someplace cool and wet. Someplace where there is lots to eat.* She thought and thought some more.

"How about the beach?" said Grab and Grub. They liked dirt, and sand was a kind of dirt.

"A beach is wet, but it is not cool," said Dab. "We would sit in the sun and get hotter and hotter."

"How about the foot of a mountain?" said Grizzle.

He liked big things. Big things made him feel small. The bigger something else was, the smaller Grizzle could feel.

Dab shook her head. "A mountain is cool, but it is not wet."

"Wherever we go, whatever we do," said Dazzle, "there must be lots to eat."

"Wherever *you* go, whatever *you* do," said Dab, "there is always a lot of

eating." But she did not sound mean.

Then Dab smiled. "I know. I know what we can do. We can go to a cool mountain. We can swim in a wet lake. We can bring lots of food and find lots of food. **We can . . . go camping!**"

So they bought a tent. They filled
five **knapsacks** full of food and
books and maps and **compasses** and
shovels and pails. They got twenty-
six men to farm-sit and cat-sit.

Then the giants climbed into their
van.

Dab was the driver. She was the
only one who fit behind the wheel.

Dazzle sat on the second seat.

Grizzle sat on the third seat. His
head stuck out of the **sunroof**.

The twins lay down in the back.
Sometimes their feet went out the

window. Sometimes their feet went out the back door.

Dab drove and drove the van. She drove until they found a big mountain. And **halfway** up the mountain, they found a big lake.

"This is just right," said Dab.

"There is no shower," said the twins.

"There is no refrigerator," said Dazzle.

"There is no *anything*," said Grizzle.

They all looked around.

But Dab held up her hand. "When

you go camping," she said, "you have everything you need. You just learn to need different things."

She took out her knapsack and opened it up.

On top was a book. It was all about camping and was called *Everything You Need.*

With the book she showed the twins how to take a shower in a **waterfall**.

She showed Dazzle how to find fresh berries on a bush.

She showed Grizzle how big and

wide and tall—and how tiny—things were in the great outdoors.

And when she was done, little Dab was very, very tired.

So she took a nap and dreamed enough stories to last the giants the rest of their camping trip.

The Hammock

The first day of the camping trip was over. Grab and Grub were tired of climbing rocks.

They were tired of swimming in the lake. They were tired of being tired.

"We want to rest," said Grab.

"A vacation *is* for resting," agreed little Dab.

"But we want to have fun resting," said Grub.

"A vacation *is* for having fun," agreed Dab.

The twins looked at each other.

They **shrugged** their shoulders.

**SHRUG. SHRUG. SHRUG.
SHRUG.**

They sighed. "How can you have
fun resting?"

"A hammock will do," said little
Dab.

"A hammock?" asked Grab.

"A hammock?" asked Grub.

"What is a hammock?" they asked together.

"Just watch," said Dab. She walked all around the camp. The twins were **confused**.

Little Dab looked at one tree. She looked at another.

At last she found two trees close together.

Sort of close. Kind of close. But not *too* close. In fact, they were

about three giant steps apart.

"This is where we will put it," said little Dab.

"The hammock?" asked Grab and Grub together.

"The hammock!" said Dab, and she smiled.

Grab looked at one tree. Grub looked at the other.

Then they **switched** places. And switched again.

"How can we put a hammock here . . . ?" asked Grab.

"Or here . . . ?" asked Grub.

"At the same time?" they asked together.

"Just watch," said Dab.

She went back into the tent, and when she came out, she carried two ropes and a huge blanket.

"That's not a hammock," said Grab. "It's a blanket."

"That's not a hammock," said Grub. "It's two ropes."

"Just watch," said little Dab.

Dab carefully tied one end of the blanket with one rope.

She tied the other end of the blanket with the other rope.

Then she tied the first rope to the first tree.

She stretched the blanket between the two trees. Finally she tied the second rope to the second tree.

"There is your hammock," Dab said. "Now get in it and rest."

"It is a swinging bed," said Grab. He climbed in.

The hammock swung around once. Grab tipped out.

He fell on the ground. **KABOOM!**

Grub laughed and laughed. "It

is a *very* swingy bed," he said.

Grub climbed into the hammock.

And fell off.

KABOOM!

Grab said, "Perhaps we should
get in together."

"Perhaps we should," said Grub.

KABOOM! KABOOM!

Grab climbed up the first tree.

Grub climbed the second tree.

They jumped into the middle of the blanket.

KAAAAAAAAABOOM!
KAAAAAAAAAABOOM!

"This kind of resting is very tiring,"

said Grab.

"But it is a lot of fun," said Grub.

Still, they had had enough. They both lay down *under* the hammock and went right to sleep.

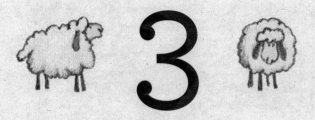

3

Dazzle's Fish

Two days of the camping trip were over.

"I'm hungry," said Dazzle. Her stomach **growled**.

"Growl," it said. And then, **"GROWL!"**

"You are always hungry," said Grizzle.

"But I am extra hungry today," said Dazzle. "Camping makes me the hungriest ever."

Dazzle looked around. Then she **gathered** all the knapsacks and opened them one by one.

She found packages of dried cereal. She found packets of dried fruit. She **peered** into the picnic basket. She saw pieces of dried beef.

"Just as I feared," she said. "Nothing to eat."

Dab shook her head. "If you do not like what we have, you must learn to live off the land."

"What does that mean?" all the giants asked.

Little Dab held up a book. It was called *Living off the Land.*

"You must pick berries. You must

find wild honey. You must catch a fish. And make a fire." Dab counted all these things on her hand.

"Berries have **prickers**," said Dazzle. "I do not want to pick berries."

"We do," said Grab and Grub.
They took a pail, and off they went,
singing a berry-picking song.

"We will find berries and
cherries galore.

"We will find raspberries,
strawberries—more!"

"Wild honey has bees," said Dazzle. "And bees . . . have stingers. I do not want to find honey."

"I do," said Grizzle. He took a bowl and went out.

And he was singing a bee-buzzing tune.

"I love to hear the wild bees buzz.

"They sing and sting, oh, just bee-cause!"

"I guess I will have to catch a fish," said Dazzle. "Fishing has no prickers. Fishing has no stingers."

She found the fishing pole. She put a hook on the line.

She made a face. "I just remembered. Fishing has worms."

"Never mind," said Dab. "I will help."

Dab went outside and came back a few minutes later with a jar full of worms that **crawled** and **sprawled**.

Dazzle made another face. Dab only laughed.

Dab and Dazzle walked down to the lake.

It was a very big lake. A giant-sized lake.

Dazzle dropped her line in and waited.

There was a little tug on the line.

Dazzle pulled. There was no fish. There was no worm either.

"I do not think I like fishing," said Dazzle. "It makes me tired. And when I get tired, I get hungry all over again."

"Never mind," said Dab. "I will put
another worm on the hook."

So Dazzle dropped her line in
again and waited.

There was another little tug on
the line.

Dazzle pulled. There was no fish.
There was no worm.

There was no hook left either.

"I *know* I do not like fishing," said
Dazzle. "Now I am even hungrier
than before."

"Never mind," said Dab. "I have

another hook. I have another worm.
This time I think you *will* catch
something."

Dazzle **grumbled,** but she dropped
in the line again.

She waited. And she waited. She
waited a long time.

There was a small tug on her line. She waited some more.

There was a bigger tug on her line. She waited even more.

Then there was the biggest tug of all.

"Pull," shouted Dab.

Dazzle pulled. She pulled and pulled and pulled and pulled out the biggest fish that she had ever seen—a giant-sized fish.

"Dinner!" shouted Dazzle.

"It's breakfast time," said Dab.

The fish looked at Dazzle. It opened

its mouth, and it closed its mouth. Its tail flapped and flopped against the ground.

Dazzle looked at the fish. She tried to think of it cleaned.

She tried to think of it cooked. She could only think of it alive.

The fish looked at Dazzle again. Its tail went up and down very slowly. Its mouth opened and closed very slowly.

Dazzle looked at the fish and felt sad. Feeling sad made her stomach hurt.

"I just remembered," said Dazzle. "I just remembered what it is that fishing has that I don't like."

"Worms," said Dab.

"No," said Dazzle. "Fish. I do not like fish."

She took the hook out of the big

fish's mouth and then picked it up by the tail. She threw the fish back into the lake, where it made a giant **SPLASH!**

The fish swam away very slowly, then faster and faster.

Dazzle and Dab walked back to camp. They had a giant-sized bowl of cereal with fresh berries and fresh honey.

They ate so much that even Dazzle was not hungry again.

Until lunch. And then she made a marvelous honey cake.

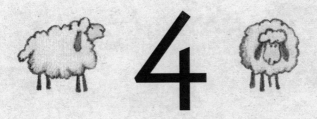

4

Grizzle's Spot

Three days of the camping trip were
over. It was early, very early, when
Grizzle woke up.

Outside the birds sang.

Outside the squirrels chattered.

He sat up in his sleeping bag. He rubbed his eyes. Then he looked around.

All the other giants were asleep and snoring.

Grizzle smiled and sniffed the air.

"Fe-fi-fo-fum, I smell the warmth of a summer sun."

He put on his walking shorts and went outside.

"Not a big walk. Not a giant-sized walk. Just a little walk," he said to himself. He was afraid he might get lost. So Grizzle began his walk.

He walked past a honey tree. He took a handful of honey.

He walked past blueberry bushes. He took a handful of blueberries.

He came at last to a little lake. He sat down by the lake.

One and two, he dipped his feet into the water.

One and two, he closed his eyes.

He began to fall asleep.

Just then Grizzle heard a noise.

It went like this: **SPLASH.**
SNORT. SPLASH. SPLASH.
SNORT. SPLASH.

Grizzle's teeth began to chatter.

It is a monster, he thought. *It is*

*coming to eat me. It is coming to
have a giant-sized meal.*

His knees began to knock. "If I
open my eyes," said Grizzle, "maybe
the noise will go away."

He opened his eyes.

SPLASH, SNORT, SPLASH!
SPLASH, SNORT, SPLASH!

The noise did not go away. The noise came nearer.

Grizzle's hands began to shake.

"If I stand up, maybe the noise will go away," he said.

He stood up. And up. And up. And up, because he was so tall.

SPLASH, SNORT, SPLASH! SPLASH, SNORT, SPLASH!

The noise was right there. Grizzle turned around to run.

He bumped into something big and **shaggy** and black.

Grizzle fell down. And down. And down.

The big, shaggy black thing licked Grizzle's blueberry hand.

Then it licked his honey hand. Its tongue was long and rough.

"Oh!" said Grizzle in a happy voice. "I thought it was a monster. But it is not. It is an enormous furry dog. Just the right size for a giant!"

The shaggy black animal shook all over. Water **splattered** Grizzle.

"Good dog. Nice dog. Come home with me," said Grizzle. "I will pet you. I will feed you. I will make you a collar. I will give you a name. Spot! I will call you Spot."

Then he giggled because the dog was all black and had no spots at all.

Grizzle held out his hands. "Come, Spot!" And Spot came right over.

Spot followed the blueberry hand and the honey hand all the way back to camp.

The other giants were wide-awake. They saw Grizzle.

They saw what followed him. **"Look out! Look out!"** cried Grab and Grub.

"There is a **humongous** bear following you," cried Dazzle.

"Do not be afraid," said Grizzle. "This is my dog. He is friendly. His

name is Spot." He sat down. The shaggy black creature sat down in Grizzle's lap. It gave Grizzle's face a huge lick.

"That is no dog," said Dab. "That really *is* a bear."

"Dog," said Grizzle.

"Bear," said Dab.

"DOG!" said Grizzle. He stood

up. And up. And up.

Whenever Grizzle stood up, he

stood up a long way.

"Dog," agreed Dab, who was big

for her age, but not *that* big!

Spot wagged his tail. He licked Dab's face with his long tongue.

Dab and Dazzle and Grab and Grub left Spot alone.

But Grizzle went over and hugged him.

He whispered into the bear's ear. "I know you really *are* a bear." He grinned. "But I know giants, too. And they would never let me keep a *bear* for a pet."

Spot rubbed up against Grizzle. He **snorted** and growled.

Grizzle snorted and growled right back.

Then they shared a big pot of honey and took turns licking it clean.

5

Going Home

It was a perfect day.

The sun was warm, but it was not hot.

The wind was cool, but it was not cold.

Fluffy white clouds hung in the sky.

The air smelled sweet. Birds sang.
Honeybees buzzed to and from
the hive.

And one very large fish flipped up
and over in the nearby lake, happy
to be alive.

"It's a perfect day," said Dab.

"A perfect day for running with a dog," said Grizzle.

"A perfect day for jumping in hammocks," said the twins.

"A perfect day for a picnic," said Dazzle.

"The perfect day to go home," said Dab.

Suddenly the perfect day was spoiled.

"Why must we go home *today*?" asked Grizzle and Grab.

"Why must we go home *today*?" asked Dazzle and Grub.

They all made unhappy faces.

Grizzle threw a rock way out into the middle of the lake, which drove angry waves onto the shore.

Little Dab took out the calendar. She pointed to the days. "This is the day we came. We put up our

tent. We made our camp." They all remembered and smiled.

"This is the day we made our hammock," said Dab to the twins.

"Do you remember?" said Grab.

"KABOOM!"

"KAAAAAAAA . . . BOOOOOOOM!" said Grub.

They both remembered and smiled.

"And this is the day we caught a fish," said Dab to Dazzle.

"That reminds me," said Dazzle. "I am hungry. But *not* for fish."

Dab turned the calendar to the next page. "And this is the day you found your bear," she said to Grizzle. "I mean your dog."

Then Dab counted on her fingers. "One day for setting up camp. One day for the hammock. One day for fishing. One day for a dog."

The other giants counted with her.

"But today we must go home.

Our twenty-six farm-sitters expect us. Our cows and sheep and horses expect us. Our cat expects us. That makes today the perfect day to go home."

But it did not seem perfect to Grizzle. He put his face in Spot's fur.

It did not seem perfect to Dazzle. She could only eat three apples and a pear. Then her stomach hurt.

It did not seem perfect to Grab and Grub. They sat on the hammock and let their feet swing slowly back and forth.

Dab shook her head. She did not
know what to do.

So she began to pack away the
camping gear all alone. It was a
big job.

The biggest!

Grizzle came over and helped by picking up the tent.

But he did not talk to Dab.

Grab and Grub helped roll up the hammock.

But they did not talk to Dab.

Dazzle helped put away the pots and pans.

But she did not talk to Dab.

Then Dab unfolded the map. She put her finger on the place where they were. Then, slowly, she moved her finger down the map to where the farm was.

Without a word, the giants climbed into their van.

They waved at Spot, who stood up. And up. And up.

He was simply huge. He waved a big, shaggy black paw.

His wave was huge, too.

Then the van started down the
road.

Down the mountain.

Along the highway.

They drove a long, long time.

Suddenly Grizzle said, "**Look!** There are our farm-sitters' houses."

He began to count them. "One . . . two . . . three . . . four . . ."

Grab and Grub said, "There is our very own fence."

Dazzle said, "I see our apple trees."

Dab said, "And there is our own Fe-Fi-Fo-Farm."

They stopped the van. They got out and looked around.

They remembered all the wonderful things waiting for them.

Their own giant beds.

Their own giant bathtubs.

Their own giant shower.

Their own giant kitchen and its enormous pantry.

And, thought Dab, *my very own bookcase filled with books.*

Then Cat came out to greet them.

"Meow," said Cat, who was the size of a tiger.

And they all agreed. It really *was* a perfect day.

A perfect day to come home.

Word List

compasses (CUHM•puhss•ez):
Instruments used for showing
direction

confused (kuhn•FYUZD): Not
sure about what to do in a situation

crawled (CRAWLD): Moved slowly
along the ground

fluffy (FLUH•fee): Light and airy

gathered (GA•thurd): Brought
together

growled (GRAULD): Made a deep,
rough sound

grumbled (GRUM•buld): Made sounds of unhappiness

halfway (HAF•way): In the middle between two places

humongous (hyu•MUN•gus): Very large

knapsacks (NAP•saks): Bags worn to carry things

peered (PEERD): Looked closely to search for something

prickers (PRIH•kerz): Sharp thorns on plant stems

shaggy (SHA•gee): Having long, rough hair

shrugged (SHRUGD): Raised shoulders to show someone doesn't know something

snorted (SNOR•ted): Pushed air through the nose

splattered (SPLA•turd): Covered with splashes or spots of something

sprawled (SPRAWLD): Spread out across an area

sunroof (SUN•roof): A small window on the roof of a vehicle that can open

switched (SWICHD): Changed or traded

vacation (vay•KAY•shun): A period of time taken off from work, school, or other activities to rest and have fun

waterfall (WHA•ter•fol): A stream of water that flows from a higher place and drops down

Questions

1. Which giants wanted to vacation at the beach?
2. Have you ever been on a camping trip? Did you sleep in a tent?
3. Have you ever used a hammock? If you didn't have a blanket handy, what else could you use?
4. Which giant does not like fishing?
5. How many days did the giants go camping?

LOOKING FOR A FAST, FUN READ? BE SURE TO MAKE IT ALADDIN QUIX!

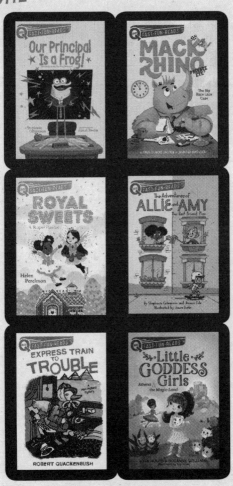

CHUCKLE YOUR WAY THROUGH THESE EASY-TO-READ ILLUSTRATED CHAPTER BOOKS!

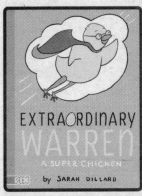

EBOOK EDITIONS ALSO AVAILABLE